Gillian Hanscombe's first sequence, *Hecate's Charms*, was published by Khasmik in Sydney in 1976. It was later scored for string quartet and voices and performed in the Wigmore Hall in London. In 1986 *Flesh and Paper*, a verse sequence written jointly with Suniti Namjoshi, was published in book and audio cassette formats by Ragweed in Canada and Jezebel Tapes and Books in England. For the cassette recording, and in a large number of performances and readings in Britain and North America, Gillian Hanscombe and Suniti Namjoshi worked with improvising musicians. Gillian Hanscombe has published several books and her poems, fiction and articles have appeared in a range of anthologies and collections mostly in feminist contexts. She has one son, lives in Devon, and now writes full-time, after earning variously as a free-lance journalist, teacher/lecturer, saleswoman, office worker, and occasional academic.

T0096588

Other books by Gillian Hanscombe:

POETRY
Hecate's Charms
Flesh and Paper (with Suniti Namjoshi)

FICTION
Between Friends

NON-FICTION
Rocking the Cradle
*The Art of Life: Dorothy Richardson and
the development of feminist consciousness*
Writing for their Lives

Sybil

The Glide of Her Tongue

Gillian Hanscombe

Assisted by the Literature Board of the Australia Council

Spinifex Press Pty Ltd,
504 Queensberry Street,
North Melbourne, Vic. 3051
Australia

First published by Spinifex Press, 1992

Typeset in 11/15 pt Times scaled 105%
        by Claire Warren, Melbourne
Production by Sylvana Scannapiego,
        Island Graphics, Melbourne
Made and Printed in Australia by The Book Printer, Victoria
Cover design: Liz Nicholson, Bite
The contents of this book have been printed
        on 100% recycled paper

National Library of Australia
Cataloguing-in-Publication entry:

CIP

Hanscombe, Gillian E. (Gillian Eve, 1945–   .)
   Sybil: the glide of her tongue

   ISBN 1 875559 05 1.

   1. Title.

A821.3

Creative Writing Program assisted by the Literature Board of
the Australia Council, the Federal Government's arts funding
and advisory body.

Australia **Council**
for the Arts

ACKNOWLEDGEMENTS

Some of these poems have appeared previously in *Up From Below: Poems of the 1980s* (Redress Press: Broadway, NSW, Australia, 1987); *Trois*, vol.3, no.3, Spring/Summer, 1988 (Laval, Québéc, Canada, 1988); *Whatever You Desire: A book of lesbian poetry* (The Oscars Press: London, UK, 1990); and *The Exploding Frangipani* (New Women's Press: Auckland, New Zealand, 1990).

These poems are for Sybil,
in all her manifestations; and for all her lovers,
devotees, followers, friends, acquaintances and back-
sliders. They are also for all her enemies, both real
and imagined.

CONTENTS

Sybil's Passacaglia 15

The Prophetical Songs 21

Sybil's Pre/texts 38

Sybil's Aggregation 48

Sybil's Reckoning 63

Sybil's Ch/arity

Patient Among Apples

From the Outside, Coming In
An Introduction

I didn't set out to become a professional lesbian; in the naïveté and passion of my adolescence – spent both wretchedly and wonderfully at a small Melbourne girls' school and then at Melbourne University – it never occurred to me that being lesbian was anything more than a personal social problem requiring well developed skills in duplicity and manipulation. It certainly never occurred to me that the word "lesbian" used as an adjective – lesbian scholar, lesbian teacher, lesbian poet – would both pathologise and marginalise anything one might do or say or think. I had no idea that the word was so powerful. My adult life has taught me that it is almost the most powerful word in the English language, capable of destroying well cemented relationships, hard-won careers, intellectual probity, emotional stability – in fact, any aspect of human affairs, from the most personal to the most public.

It became clear, finally, that this word "lesbian" does – all by itself – change reality. It is an awesome word. I have learned to respect it. I know it can't be used casually, like Australian, or writer, or mother, or any of the other words I can use about myself in the ordinary ways everyone else uses them. I know it is a deeply serious word – so serious that, like the old name for God, the superstitions and taboos and dreads decree that it should never be uttered at all, and should definitely never be spelt out. That has been my experience of the world.

When I took courage from the new feminism and began to take this word to myself, publicly and generally, I found myself gathered up, welcomed and embraced into a new life, a new reality. I was among hundreds of women, thousands – if you count in all the readers and conference-attenders and friends of friends and friends of their friends – for whom the positive power of the word was a liberation and a promise of life and freedom and energy quite as profound as anything that could happen to any potential saint on the road to Damascus. We lesbians were still shunned, feared, pitied, hated, mocked or threatened by mainstreamers; but we had each other. And the ghetto we shared we made beautiful with our sounds and scents, our movements and music, our dreams, our plans, our life histories – but above all, with our words. For a time we found bliss in our newly created Eden. It was a while before the serpent entered, bearing the promise of our full humanity clearly upon her features.

It's thirty years, now, since I first heard the word lesbian and understood that it had singled me out. It has blessed me with the love of women. It has cursed me with the weaknesses of the scapegoat, the outsider and the victim. It has honoured me with the vision of a more evolved, a more civilised humanity.

What we lesbian women have to say, we say most directly to each other, since lesbians have the best reasons of all for understanding quickly and willingly what is being said. But our language, being human, is not meant to resound only within the spaces we have made for ourselves. What we say is as important and significant for anyone who can hear it as have ever been the songs and stories, the poems and expositions, the theories and histories that our various cultures venerate. We have important things to say about love, hope, despair, about birth and death, about systems of knowledge, about pain, about mystery. We have, that is (to use the jargon of the organisational and managerial bureaucracies), leadership potential.

Sybil – The Glide of Her Tongue is my way of focusing and feeling and perceiving these things. In 1985, I went with Suniti Namjoshi to Greece and took a day trip to Delphi. It was a blue Mediterranean day, spring-hot and slightly out of season. Mount Parnassus shimmered, the olive trees – never young-looking to the foreign eye, so gnarled and twisted they are — glittered and shone. The sea in the distance, separating the mainland from the Peloponnesus, was an astonishing cobalt blue. The guide explained this and that as we spiralled up through the magic rubble towards the temple. Suniti remarked that she hadn't expected to find the old religion dead, because in India, the broken carvings, the rocks made into gods and shrines, the ruined temples – whether centuries old or made yesterday – still take and give all the secrets of ardour. The guide rehearsed how the ancients believed this spot to be the navel of the world. And it was, that day, for me. It truly was. How like a lesbian the sybil was, speaking plain (why should we think otherwise?), but being heard in riddles.

A lesbian, like the sybil, lives out of time, out of place, out of history. She is an aberration. Her social identity is factitious – a grotesquerie some-how accommodated at dinner parties, at weddings and funerals, in workplaces, on census forms. I claim the sybil because there are thousands of us who also want to tell the truth: to each other; and to anyone.

The myth tells us that the sybil supplanted the older pythoness, who spoke in the days of the matriarchal cosmology when goddesses ruled. When patriarchy pushed the goddess religion aside, the sybil was set up under the provenance of Apollo. It is like that for us: what a lesbian speaks will be tolerated by patriarchal men and women because what she says can be heard as riddles, as non/sense, as half/witted, as something needing re-interpretation.

Writing these poems has involved giving utterance to the many lesbian voices inside my head which belong either to my own personal history, or to the details of other lesbian lives, or to our collective experiences. The voices are heterogeneous: there is she of the bars and discos (wanting love); and she of the exhibitionistic ghetto (wanting love); and she of the moralising movement (wanting love); and she of the history-gatherers (wanting love); and she who is mistress of the bed (wanting love); and she who sits apart, mourning and meditating, who understands love, and can therefore give it. The voices have demanded, for the most part, first that I formalise their vying claims into dialogues; and next that I de-formalise the verse structures of my past. So Sybil appeared, uttering for all of us under cover of prophecy; and moving her lesbian presence, both sweetly and angrily, clothed in virtues, cloaked in vices, through all our histories, past and to come. She speaks both to us and for us, and is therefore at once both austere and sensual, impassioned and weary, admirable and shameful. She tells us what we know already, what we know about, what we'd rather not know at all.

The sequence is divided into eight sections. The first, "Sybil's Calling", offers the experience of being called: the experience of name-calling and scapegoating, at one extreme; and of vocation, at the other. "Sybil's Saturation" deals with the accretions, both individual and collective, of the outrageous fortunes that have been, and remain, integral to the destinies of lesbians. "Sybil's Passacaglia" uses as a metaphor a musical form which gives order and unity through repetition and variation: lesbian knowledge, that is, has its own assembly of litanies and reiterations. "The Prophetical Songs" emphasise the dilemma all lesbians face when they try to relate and integrate their particular insights and feelings into the general human tapestry. "Sybil's Pre/texts" explores the two-edged sword of authority and responsibility, on the one hand, and the possibilities for redemption, on the other. "Sybil"s Aggregation" addresses the moral minefield of what may/may not happen to the patriarchs under a lesbian dispensation. What is permissible? What is right? Is what is permissible the same thing, anyway, as what is right? "Sybil"s Reckoning" uses as a metaphor the free market philosophy which is the most recent of the cancerous contributions offered by patriarchal capitalism to the furtherance of the collective "good". We lesbians are implicated in getting and spending and improving our position. But what are the real costs? And can we afford them? The final section, "Sybil's Ch/arity", says love is the only possible law; but it is a complex law, and not unproblematic. The hiatus indicated by the stroke / breaks the word in two, and is meant to mark hesitation when the word "charity" is said aloud. The foundations of wisdom and religion do, in the end, demand even more than truth-telling – they demand contrition and compassion.

There will be those who find this sequence alienating, finding the forms of the poems too loose, or the language too dense, or the themes too ambiguous, or the judgements too harsh, or the invitations too hidden. I apologise sincerely to those readers and listeners. No poet sets out deliberately to obscure, or intending to write something dense and difficult. I have written as clearly as I can; and I have said what I see and hear and feel with as much focus as lies within my present capacity. It is currently fashionable in some readerships, including some feminist ones, to argue that literature should be "accessible", by which is meant a challenge to those stances called élitist, or anti-egalitarian, or just plain arrogant. Of course I want what I write to be accessible. That isn't, however, entirely within my control. The reader's willingness, openness and interest are as essential to the meaning of a text as is the poet's obligation to tell the truth.

In the poem "Wanted to play highjinx/minx, didn't you?", for example ("The Prophetical Songs", 13), it isn't immediately obvious that Sybil, in her guise as know-all, power-tripper and competitor, is letting me (and all of us) know that *she* knows what's what. It isn't immediately obvious – but it is obvious. She knows the persecutions suffered by a lesbian girl; but she knows, as well, the consequent dangers of self-pity. She points out that such girls do, after all, win other girls, who later, come of age, find a woman in their turn. Wasn't the persecution worth it? Do we not, whatever the cost, give thanks? Or take the next poem, "I might (says Sybil) if pressed" ("The Prophetical Songs", 14), which presents the lesbian's ambivalence about the personal meaning of heterosexuality. It seems less real, less profound, less convincing, somehow implausible as a woman's authentic choice (when there is enormous pressure, how can you *tell* what is submission and what is free choice?). Less real it may be: but it is also such a threat. A woman may simply *be* less authentic and may happily give herself up. Sybil, like many of us, so many times, must comfort herself alone if her woman deserts to the patriarchy. Or in the final poem, "Sometimes Sybil slides about", it's clear that the law of love isn't, by its nature, clear and straightforward. On the one hand, love must persist, since only through love can the world be redeemed. On the other hand, what is the difference between the pursuit of love and "taking what you want"? And how does anyone actually tell the difference? Can anything ever by purged by martyrdom? Or merely stained by it? What, therefore, can we make of lesbian martyrdom? If we claim the world, are we not also – very fundamentally – of the world?

I have become persuaded, writing this sequence, that Sybil's chief virtue is her tremendous and terrifying endurance. She endures anything and everything, from glory to corruption, from passion to pettiness, from retribution to redemption. That endurance is what all lesbians know. It is written, in countless codes and histories and songs and symptoms and dialects and litanies, in the secrets of our flesh. It has been our major contribution to the civilising of ourselves and it is also our continuing contribution to the civilising of the whole species that remains to be done.

Like my fellows, I owe nearly everything I value to the ebbing and flowing offered me by lovers, friends, colleagues, students and a few of my kin, and, more distantly, to the larger networks who are part of Sybil's circle. Particularly, though, I owe special gratitude to Susan Hawthorne and Renate Klein of Spinifex, for their good faith; and to Suniti Namjoshi, for her friendship and for her love.

G. H.
Rousdon, Devon
October 1991

Sybil's Calling

Did they plant her? and did she, therefore, grow like a stone?
  Or was she merely a refugee?
Having saluted her, did they hide in her skirts?
Did she doom them to reverence?
  I hang my head and remember her glamour.

1

Sybil was overcome by sulphur, they say now. We dykes trailed dumbly in the wake of the demolition squads. The fissure of dead earth's lips is long since settled back to stone and the words are in the air only, only at Parnassus. It is necessary to make pilgrimage. Being anciently outcast, we heard what was in the air, felt the sun on the crumbs of Delphi, saw olives and cypresses flare.

2

At three-and-thirty she sipped coffee in cafés. There were people all about, but they were all fish. There were buildings, all made of water. There were policemen (their white claws drawn, in and out, in and out, plastic cars in their mouths, crunch). There was a priest (checking his cassocked phallus; checking, checking).There were vendors, fur slicked down, noses twitching after carrots.

Flowers there were in window-boxes, in wire baskets, in pots and buckets, everywhere in park-beds (washed and polished) and in brick-dust (all triumphant).

Well, the country then, thought Sybil. (Women with shining skin, women with lusts, women who know flesh from grass.) I shall sit on a mountain. I shall speak when I'm asked. I shall be to my lover a pillar of salt, a pillar of fire. We'll make love in the open, sharing the cypresses, staining the bracken. We'll sin, even.

When Sybil went to Parnassus, she was thirty-three; and not yet a grandmother.

3

Sybil struggled with the satisfaction of knowledge, remembering the queen who knew how to dress and how to boss everyone. The queen ruled; the men were exhausted. Day and night they did what she said. The women she kept busy with adoring each other. (The children? Oh, they went to school as children do; and became women and men as everyone must.) The animals played about and never dreamed of killing each other. (But what did they eat? Eat? Oh, the men fed them.)

After long ages, the queen grew bored. She was jaded with success. They ought to be grateful, she thought with resentment.

This is the true history of the world; how the good queen died without issue; how the women and men turned in towards one another. Animals took to the forest, turned savage, and preyed where they could. It was unforgivable, surely (Sybil wondered), to use a queen like that . . . .

4

I mean, if you'd been a mother or a lover (or a mother and a lover) in a cavern in a canyon, excavating for a minefield, why then, perhaps you'd be found as well at the top of a cypress, halfway up Parnassus, screeching like a phoenix; and you'd see the people in their robes and garments, their silks and velvets, their tatters and insignia (uniformed all), ambling underneath and going about the ways of the world; and occasionally glancing up and wondering to each other why that bird was going on and on and what about. And if you'd seen what she – in her vices and capacities – was made to see, why then, you wouldn't need me to explain at you about the climate and about the heat and rain, up and down the mountain till the leaves turn metal. Oh, birds can talk sometimes. Anything is possible.

5

Sybil grew on the great mountain and we knew that's where we had to go. She was always for us, though the others tucked their heads down, out of sight. So much for gods. And mortals? . . . it seemed to them the best thing was to drug her night and day. They said she was theirs, that she spoke their words, that she spoke for them; but we knew just the same. She comes twice in our lives: in our preknowing and in the confirmation. As we garland her feet, we adore and desire.

Sybil's Saturation

No one is proud of dykes (not families not neigh-bours not friends not workmates not bosses not teachers not mentors not universities not literature societies not any nation not any ruler not any benefactor not any priest not any healer not any advocate). Only other dykes are proud of dykes. People say live and let live but why should we?

1

In a dell dingle copse edge of a wood in England, a dyke can look out of place, clutter up the scenery, put askew the symmetry. By contrast with any lover and his lass, she can seem hell-bent on disruption for the sake of . . . of . . .

though she thinks (poor she) she imagines she's there like any lover and his lass, for the view. The trouble is, perhaps, that any lover and his lass think, who is she? to be on her own, so alone, so lacking for company? or else, who are they, two together, like that? And she (and the two of them together) don't think about what a lover and his lass are thinking. They make that quite clear.

"And how do you dare" – suddenly it's said, in a dell dingle copse edge of a wood in England, it's said, because a lover and his lass are raging now – "to be like that, like that?"

So she (and the two together; and we) take out compasses and check the latitude, study the season, look up history, recite poetry, consult government and universities, scan logic and religion.

Remember Sybil. Is it different at Parnassus where the world bisects? Do the dykes walk unremarked? And are we therefore less discerning?

2

Yes doctor we admit we confess we are often troubled we have visitations we are possessed of devils we have dreams and portents we speak in tongues we hear voices we hallucinate we levitate we have fantasies we have memories we have longings we see visions of the deaths of men.

3

So, Sybil, might we together answer? We haven't died. Why don't we abolish the hideaway houses the walled gardens where girls make love among poppies and lady lovers tend hibiscus? When the gardens were planted, women of pleasure abolished men altogether and mated only in season. (I say come when you say pain when you say rage I receive your breasts.) And they kept their babies for tomorrow. (My hands are fish my head is a young ewe butting.)

4

We could abolish assemblies and scripted complaints. And we could abolish fashion again; relent in the grim cause of individual incident, of the divisions of the freedom to dissent; and come again to the collective supper not knowing who is for us and who against.

5

Let's abolish apples, figs, garden tools, the worm that turns, the two-by-two who (hand in hand) lay claim to every garden in the land and let's investigate the state of the union said to unify the State.

6

. . . and then we might abolish rhetorical devices,
confessional rites, conventional rights (you see how
one's mind wanders: you say rage and I say pain
and you say oppression and I say again and you
say all-men-are-rapists and I say amen) and abolish
tourist cathedrals with their gold plate padlocked
and their pretty boys (treble and descant) breathing
and vaulting back and forth for recording technicians
on overtime

        abolish mimicry, refrain, repeats of
cold sheep on February hills, all artful works from
our ministrations our administrations.

7

No beasts ourselves, we live among beasts (swift and muscled, fanged and fit, hunters in hordes, flesheaters); we've learned to tread lightly, to tunnel in burrows, even to fly. We're always changing. When we sense the burn in our eyes, we freeze them in ice and when fur pricks through our skin, we tear it out. Claws we keep trimmed, teeth we keep filed and blunt, horns we keep out of sight. We walk upright, feel tall; and hide with dignity. (We've discussed the choice: to be brave and flayed or be coiled and craven, spat upon, patient among apples.)

Sybil's Passacaglia

In caves and corridors I crouch. No noonday sun for me, no incandescent light. I festoon me with smoke and shadows. I gave up well-tempered phrasing for the sake of her pleasure – and hers, and hers –

I descended into speech.

1

Sybil prefers, when permitted, to shun the spotlight. She knows, better than we've been taught, the problems of prophecy, the splendour of stardust. Women who walk tall are liable to be brought low and made to service the gods. In the deviousness of her heart, therefore, she strings her words with practised aforethought, mesmeric by default. To those who can hear, she speaks plain: let women who pair dare more than dally, dare more than defy; let women who pair prescribe the new order. When she mutters under sulphur, Sybil rehearses the voices of millions.

2

It's got to the stage, after all, where no woman can sit down to write her record with her hand over her figleaf. There's the sacking of the Vatican to be done; and the remaking of America. China waits; and India. Africa sits on the brink. And there are all those stories to face.

Sybil waits also. You can hear her waiting. You can hear how she hears (oh, you can tell me your visions. You usually do. In any case, I have my own to contend with. And I know you've done such a lot of round-the-corner and over-the-fence and under-the-counter. I know how difficult it is without power and money and status which, being attained, validate.

But I must admonish you, since you ask. You've made certain choices.)

(Art, anyway, is an alibi, don't you see?)

3

In between the hieroglyphs, a horse-laugh. (Well, how would you feel, stuck on a three-legged stool to be gawked at, the men pretending to hang on every word and all the time just sizing up the cost-effectiveness of followings . . .?)

Do you know what I'm really thinking?

Oh, I've got breasts all right and decent flanks and wetness to cover you with. I'm not just mind over matter, not just sulphurous babblings. I'm eyeing you up; and after, I'll feel where I can.

And as for you, flaunting your womanly ways and wondering whether I'd dare, whether I scare easy, I'll tell you what you're wondering: that I know as well as you the sweat, the wet, the tonguing and handling and the starting over.

Like all women, I'll tend to the worshipful men for my life's sake, and give them mouthings to muse on; but my eye is on you, my woman of the gilded limbs, and after my mouth come hands.

4

There, says Sybil, watch them go, untoward, inelegant: hims and hers, blacks and whites, straights and dykes, doing the two-step, never bored. There's rich and poor, us and them, Irish and not, Jewish and not, Third World and not, American and not (seascapes, landscapes, landed interests, vested interests) disabled on one count, disabled on all counts. There's (Thatcher, South Africa, the Middle East, Central America, Ethiopia, Soviet imperialism, American imperialism, fundamentalism, food mountains, unemployment, sweated labour, irradiation, pollution, deforestation, corruption, multinationals, Swiss bankers, monarchy, atrophy, militant nationalism, white supremacy, terrorism, drug addiction) plenty going on

never boring.

And there's you and me, my sweet duality.

5

Back in the garden (between utterances) where
we're (bent on) existing oh well we lay out phrases
thin down rows of sentences (they must be cleaned
they must be vacuum-packed for supermarkets) we
subvert the weather with all manner of devices
(pleats to the knee and nipples altogether hidden)
because the sisters require to know the authentic
pain, the acceptable ethic (the origin of idioms, the
precise inflection) so that words betoken neither
governed nor governing

                      and if flaws nevertheless
appear, our Rule allows no unpicking of syntax
without confessional credentials (she says pain I
was – and I say rage because –)

                                and so shall we
ever love one another

The Prophetical Songs

To the ancient of days, queen of heaven and of all the worlds beneath and of all my lives done and to come, greetings.

I bring what I sing; and she whom you licensed sings likewise. Above, between and beneath is your due.

1

After abolition, Sybil may come. She is a girl. She is a dragon. A dragongirl. Sybil is a grandmother, aged forty-nine. Her daughters are aged twenty-eight. Sybil is a goat. An experienced she-goat. She is a trademark. A hard sell.

Sybil has always been all-girl. When she is young, she flies like a sphinx, she roars like a lioness in the circles of the stars. Often she runs her kingdom from coffeeshops, makes us fly and cry (bidden and driven, eyes red as coals from adoring all night.)

We keep our vows, spy for her everywhere. Man the Man, King of Kings, broke his lance on her thigh and hunts her to the death. Let the law go hang.

Sybil has run up her account to a gasping height. Her sins are scarlet and white, are green with rust, are black as sea at night. Her desires divine her. In the end, even her belly she has filled by herself.

2

She whom I honour, honoured me. Therefore I
speak. Disregard all rumours you may have heard.
I never speak in riddles: that's simply what men
hear.

(Oh, she is agile, strong-handed, supple and
insistent. She is handsome. She shines in the dark.
My breasts fall by themselves into her hands.)

Love
is a discipline, she told me; and must be learned.

3

In the guise of Artemis, hunter, you can ride me all the way to the sun; and be ridden back again. Your bow-arm is stronger than an olive-stump, though your hands are as smooth as plums. When you pour libations, my ears sting with the brim and swish of your words. I adore the bowstring pulled taut; the symptoms of desire.

4

Does she know
        when she's standing, speaking
        (gowned and silky)
so unlikely maybe or
untimely in this public circumstance
        that (how) I romance?
I admit I mean to undo,
unfasten, in my own presence also standing, smiling,
for my own enhancing.
        (Naked most fluent, better than
any divine drapery; and excellently skilled.)
As fictive as a hologram, you might reply.
But I, who have held all manner of flesh and grass,
        defiant ferns, fish even,
        and the whack of unkind water,
willingly commit idolatry.
        Does she know
when she's standing, speaking
with what unlikely images
        I must contend?

5

The sea breasted herself, reared, fell, and was fooled. Later, she lay flat and brooding. If I had a grain of greatness in me, I'd call her a god and be glad. I'd prepare ceremonies.

But I know better. I know she herself fawns at the come-hither of our-lady-the-moon. (My lover, who also has a secret face, beckons nightly. I beckon in my turn. We were both, long ago, imprinted by tides.)

6

I shall lie me down by my Ladye
and practise symmetry
I shall raise me up when the gulls cry
and learn idolatry.

I shall stalk through the world sans Ladye
and pay for amity
I shall meditate in the flamelight
and master mimicry.

7

I looked upon the rising storm
with equanimity
what could it do to me or mine,
that mad, unruly sea?
And then, within my walls, I watched
my own advance on me.

8

By rule of thumb I come gracefully, bearing gifts.
There is thrift in the teasing, prudence in pleasing,
restraint in remembrance of passion.
                                    I glance and
                    glitter; I laugh the laugh of cut glass.
                                    As I leave the bed
I remark how you see me lose glamour, gain gravity.

9

She dared more than roses,
than pruning gloves,
      or a still-life stance
      or a boastful camera;
for me she dared blood on the tongue,
thorns in the bower of bliss.
When I kiss her hand,
      she forgives my intentions.

10

Want to let fly, little hushabye, while the bird's on
the wing? Will you try anything?

Or pretend to rest easy?

It takes some making
to stay firm and clean and not let on how you're
driven. (It isn't getting a woman right between the
eyes that satisfies. It's the reconciling pain.)

I'll
come again when you're deep in the remembering.
Meanwhile take care. There's a flock of feathered
women in the air.

11

After we'd decided, we made promises. And after
that, we kept them. And after that came the failures.
Then we got down to it: mapped each other's flaws,
and confessed to chivalry. And then, because of all
that, we made love with our bare hands. Outside,
the pigeons pecking at the moss on the roof, were
also contented.

12

When that the sweet wind will blow or go meddling among the grasses so that even the sheep (who can stand anything) are beguiled and unseasonally persuaded and run mad to their slaughter (we kept a good table, my women and I, until they said that even the women must stand and be counted) – well, I admit that the panic will be shocking. The women will sweat and swear like men. The sun will boil. The rain will scald the earth's belly. No matter; because of each idyll, comes desire.

13

Wanted to play highjinx/minx, didn't you? with a crown of thorns . . . . wanted to get it well done, to get it all down in case they came home early . . . wanted to tell her how it really is/was, didn't you? the authorised version.

Well, I made sure you didn't and can't, since you won't bow down and play reverence.

Don't hiss at me or implore how you wanted more, how mother made you pray how teachers said obey how doctors said away with her (far away) how grown girls giggled when they saw; and don't tell me how Heavenly Father threatened fire.

When you were young, there was a girl called Glory who couldn't anything: she couldn't sing, she couldn't sew, she couldn't read or write or calculate, she couldn't win at sports, or conjure mysteries, or specially cook and clean; but she could string the boys about her and thus be queen. And the fathers said what a pretty pretty girl, what a very pretty thing.

And you took her, didn't you, when you thought I wasn't looking. Without my consent. Now you know I've known all along how you got Glory in the middle of her womaning and how I envied you and made you pay.

Praise be.

14

I might (says Sybil), if pressed, construct the narrative of how the love of women undercuts a multitude. You know how life's invented. For every she, a he made mad and lordly. But that's just seeing. Underneath the sea, where there's believing, are the mermaids breathing as we dream. I've heard how our days since earth began are numbered and batched in secret. At times, even I forsake my women. But now let's admit how things are. Whoever says she's his, may do so for his heart's content. We're not here to spend ourselves in repudiation. (She, to herself only, murmurs her desire.)

15

As far as Sybil is concerned, there's no problem. Indeed, there shouldn't be a problem. Let the people sing, she mutters; let them dance. The musicians are ready, serving-girls waiting; the sisters in their green and fluent robes are right on hand. There's light and space. Plenty of warmth. They're all still young and guileless. Nor will there be ever again a rainbow splitting the heavens.

16

For in the sweet and future fires
where devils leap and angels magnify,
partaking equally in courtesy
(each woman worthy of her hire),
it's found right, in the end, to simplify,
deleting in order: men and children first,
women second best, and last
the goddess with her lyre.

                          Starting over
is the least of our desire.

Sybil's Pre/texts

Sybil named the stars we see, a billion light
                                        years back;
Later, the fall of man was blamed on woman;
And fallen women were blamed on the serpent;
And the serpent was blamed on the mind of god
                                        (wherein he lay);
And god took flesh and Aphrodite rose from
                                        the waves.

The earth breathes fire and sulphur still;
And Sybil has her way.

1

England is sick. It's dead. Lie down and play dead, pretty England. That's what the creatures do when they're out-bruted. We've got you. You're dead. It's said that dykes were the primary infestation; but some of them bred, and were therefore permitted. Others played mongrel, and fawned. What harm could they do? They were left to belong. A few wrote books, held meetings, clapped their hands. Who, though, could they stay or sway? No, no, it's England that died; it's the spirit of man that's sick and plays dead. You're mad, lazy England: you took all of history and invented it, and yet you lie stricken, digesting yourself. You'd like the margins checked? Ah well. We heard what you wrote so we took down those words. You'll find us in Boston, in Delhi and Cape Town, in Melbourne, Nairobi, Hong Kong, Fiji; we're in Montreal even (we've started translations). Don't fret, dear old England, most merciless fatherland; lie down, O most fortunate. You're sick. You're dead.

2

Some people will believe anything: Adam and Eve, quantum theory, the rights of the rich. There are priests, of course, and military technicians, looting and lying. (It may not be moral and we're sorry for our sins, but at least they're natural.)

There are those who turn to me. What am I supposed to do? I declare my interest. Women loot less, having learned submission; and if we lie, it's done in good faith (and is anyway in our best interest.) But what if they catch me in my acts of adoration? Shall I smile benignly? Catch as catch can?

(For the heat of her thighs I cast oceans aside. For the presence of her breasts I forsake cities. For the glide of her tongue I undo dynasties. Even so, I sit contented. I watch the seawaves greenly rising.)

3

Being dykes, we adore in the dark, feel well within our walls. History never penetrates us straight, nor cleaves us navel to chaps

it seeps in sideways enters in whispers oozes when we're distempered craves (that is) attention. We pick what we can seed and garden by night.

We know our one anothers; we can see each secret eye, each set of hardened hands/and the ears pricked, scanning the static. (Fellow gallants and gardeners, giants, lovers, fellow followers, we ripen one by one and two by two.)

Being dykes, we show each other cities (not ours) decked with paintings (not about us) filled with families (whose blood we share but who regret).

Being dykes, we're not to be trusted.

Our cause is rude.

But watch: we know alchemy, turn base things into gold.

4

Said songs are a luxury (us glad and gaudy) better to suffer give voice to anger better to let go let fly do some damage somewhere better to fly better to be better.

5

She tells us her history and we unravel.
She tells us our history which she unravels.
She tells us the history they've made.
She asks us what we make of history.
We tell her we've noticed in the
    textbooks guidebooks concentration-camp
                    memorials
    how we're not mentioned.
So there you are, she says comfortably.

6

Sybil said sorry said sorrily with a sweetening grace that she's raced by the suffering sisters, turned left at the equal pay headquarters, trekked left again at the nurseries campaign stall, sped hard down the other side of the street sensing the abortion march coming/said sorrily that she'd finally blown sky-high to spy down faster than civil rights illuminate

(where are the derelict paths and passages, the leaking basements and the upper rooms of publicans, the shabby bookshops and the tinselled nightclubs where the women-only hide and fling?)

I want, said Sybil (sorrowful as sunlight on a virgin land) more than altarfire and general com-mination/or, the logic of repair: I want a genuine despair.

7

Whether or not the white chrysanthemum provided ecstasy and whether or not the high buildings could perform their lachrymosa and whether or not the tall people threw down their spears in Leicester Square or at Parnassus made, in the end, no difference. Whatever selection had been involved was dictated by the impulse to shape and by the despair of re/making the world. Sybil, having cut loose from the institutions that first invented her, was faced with imperatives: clear lines; and satisfaction.

There was no torment in the woman's face, there in the next car, speeding; nor any spite in the bitching of pigeons, raucous among crumbs.

There is only once; there is only the resurrection of the past in the ruthless pursuit of history.

Having cut loose, Sybil is become glorious (though she sprang from an undistinguished province, from family sins more ancient than four generations). Because she kissed the girls she loved and shared their breasts and ransacked willingly among their thighs, she learned to speak code and eclipse, to speak honeysuckle and rosemary, to speak old wine.

8

All things generally await redemption. The daffodils
particularly now are sorry
      turn in habit to the sky
          (they've bruised her puffy
face all grey and yellow) (more in sorrow than in
                          anger).

Sybil weeps to know such trumpetings.

9

We ripen and ripen and ripen (and fall to the ground
and seed . . . . and multiply) over and over and
over.

Sybil's Aggregation

Let us reason together, my child:
> *you speak;*
> *I shall translate.*
The whole world (can I help it?)
is patterned after my configurations.

1

I, Sybil, for the second time, for the second time of asking, speak and am bespoken. In the night of the long knives, I come to bury my dead. I've buried them before: in urns and boxes, by rivers, by landmarks. I have performed rituals as often as was seemly. I can

remember the scented ti-tree in the south; and the fine fir forests of the north. Ashes upon ashes I have sifted and scattered. And I've cried at full pitch from the tops of mountains; no one has cried longer. But still my dead unbury themselves, return to my unwelcome arms; still they implore, and suckle, and hiss. In my

bower of bliss, I prepare libations. This is (I hear myself pronounce) neither magic nor madness. They are (after all?) my own dead, and may not be abandoned.

2

It was luxurious, says my father, to feel my arm end in a fist, to hear my deeps roar swell through the whole house, to spread this chest wide as a bass drum that can be beaten with whatever frenzy and never break. I never

thought of hormones; I thought it was all me. Who would have thought, says my father (rhetorically, no answer required) – who would have thought, says my father (diseased and dying) – that that great bully would come to this?

My duty is to order the winding sheet and to make other preparations. I rest easy, having loved him not. So may he return. So may I, with this urn, sift and filter, cover and scatter.

In England, for piety, they grow rosebeds.

3

I, Sybil, have put no torch to living flesh and am
therefore guiltless. Being incapable makes me
unculpable.

Therefore I can hear your confession.
Speak gently and in sentences. If you need to cry
out, you must find ocean beds, you must find
crevasses, you must slide through deserts. If you
want to cry out, you must confine yourself to danger.
We are preoccupied here with sentences that make
sense.

4

We were roaming in the gloaming, says my father
(in the spirit of his times). We had hearts as strong
as horses, we had pickaxes for friends. We tamed
the land, we shamed our foes, we bred like bulls, we
wept with pride when we saw our own brotherhood.
It was a mystery how we wept and felt.

I, Sybil, sicken at my roots and wither fast.

5

From the unburying of the dead, my sister, make
what is pleasing. Make from these ashes castles
and carparks, inheritance laws, degrees in history.
Be unbound, be careful and faithful. Above

all, my
sister, say it with gardens. In India (for example),
the wealthy say it with sandalwood.

6

Why, says my father, is it irrelevant that I did my duty? I was a provider. I was a protector. I was a success.

So I made mistakes. Am I therefore disqualified? More than?

So I was arrogant. Self-indulgent. Insincere. So I was a pretender.

So?

7

I, Sybil, love no man. Then let the gods rend me. And I, Sybil, love no womanly woman. Then let the goddess cast me out. And I, Sybil, have eaten meat and have loosed cattle into wild pastures and have watched forests burn for the sake of stock exchanges and sentences.

And I, Sybil, have burned with hatred for my sisters until I held my charred heart hot in my hands and still I have gone on living.

Bless me sisters for I have sinned. On the high mountains there is blood in the snow and a great cry crying.

8

I am, you might have guessed, obsessed; but that is no matter. In my second time of asking there has been less scenery. The language has moved on and has become more (or less) precise. New words must deliver not what is heard or felt, but what is quantifiable.

Make from the ashes what is beautiful; not, first, the songs or poetry, since they come freely and by grace. Make, first, the market plan and next its calculations.

When the gods and goddesses lay dead, we gave them decent burial. And when the saints lay dead, we wished them well. And when our fathers died, we threw our mothers on the pyres and blessed them fervently. Soon we shall make dead our own offspring. And dead are we already to democracy and desire.

(Even so, freely and by grace, come songs and poetry.)

9

See, says my father, these sisters you espouse you
have betrayed. How, then, can you demand ascen-
dancy? By what ethic have you left me here,
coffined and condemned, since I, like, you speak in
sentences?

      (Not the bloodline, you may understand,
nor superstitious laws – but the fellow-feeling, don't
you see?)

10

I say it with sandalwood and rosebeds. I say it with angels' wings. I say it with mud and ashes. I say it with shovels and cement-mixers. I say it with famine relief. I say it with paid-up mortgages and garden maintenance. I say it with votes and letterheads. I say it with the best music in the best concert halls. I say it with hair-shirt and chains.

What more do you want?

11

Coming to terms, O king, means: you sin, and I pay. Not that you think of it as sinning; more playing, or doing what comes naturally.

I put it to you: how important is intention?

(Coming to terms means some things can't be bought. Rage, for example, is unenhancing, cannot make decorous, will not deck the burnished skies with beauty.)

I put it to you: how important needed you to be?

There was a girl, you know, who undertook immensities, tracing her ignorant body's lines with the sacred fire. No wonder, then, you may remark, if the fire refines.

When the house was filled with smoke came six-winged seraphim, bearing living coals with which to bless my lips. Thus kissed, was my iniquity undone. This method of becoming, you understand, may not take place in a woman's temple, since her gods cannot help but desire her.

Fathers, by definition, suffer the pangs of unchildbirth. Why, therefore, are you continually astonished?

12

And after travelling, the rewards of home-cooking and the neighbours round for the news. Aw, says my father, happy with his souvenirs, I have seen the world and there are no dragons or unicorns, and money talks anywhere.

Aw, says my father: the cruise down the Rhine was spectacular. There was the rock where the Lorelei sang, and the band played on. But there's nowhere (says my father, with his mouth half full of oysters and wine on his bib) – there's nowhere like Us/tralia.

Pain, I learn, is something only foreigners can feel.

13

Full six feet my father lies, but I rest uneasy. I know nothing of swords and hatchets, nothing of smiting the Amalakites, nothing of swooping down from the hills, nothing of laying the flex and setting the timer. But I had a cause; I had the cause of causes. Let oh let the patriarch die, and I shall flourish. I shall let down my hair. I shall swell with babies, year after year, and I shall place them on rocks for the she-wolf to find; I shall float them down rivers; I shall put them in rockets to find outer space. I shall cover myself with beauty and seek renown.

Full six feet my father lies. He does nothing to prevent me. He likes my style.

14

I hesitate to think it, but . . . my father may not be
the worst. There's a sad/bad woman called Leila-
phone in London. She

                                    gathers the sisters and smiles
at them with her teeth. At night she decapitates
frogs and sets them dancing. She says there are
many roads to Rome. She likes whips and knives
and nipple rings. She says, as well, that frogs are a
tool of the patriarchy.

Sybil's Reckoning

the women have become armies they are
unstitching the syntax it is
irrevocable they never stop not
even to eat and drink.
                              We
may not speak of it
                    even the
verbs are tipped with poison
                         if I am
heard I shall be
flayed and stretched out to dry
                         and the
words are being
rewoven back to front and
therefore I am lost to you

1

In my modulations between ecstasy and devotion
                                        I have
found the pearl of great price.
What is distinctive about this pearl is that there is
no other like it.
                In
free market philosophy, this
phenomenon relates to supply and demand.
I am conditioned to reject price fixing;
therefore this pearl is kept secret
in the talisman box in my attic.

2

In the marketplace (here is a riddle) sits the seller of plaited onions (Save the Environment, Your Grace!); and the seller of handwoven fabrics (Save the Third World, Your Grace!); and the seller of money itself (Save the Money Supply, Your Grace!). They are three good women; all must survive. They encourage competition and accept prizes. All must survive. They husband their resources and study politics. They complain hardly at all.

But you must choose who is most worthy: there is only one true religion; only one gold medal; only one kidney machine; only one publishing house; only one mother; only one day left; only one friend.

You must choose, so that one, at least, may prosper. But having chosen, you are guilty of arrogance and must do penance. Your penance is a seat in the marketplace. You will be a seller of souls.

3

Remind me, Sybil, how the women flocked to
overcome, but how – being birds of a feather –
they fought over every crumb.

I shall commit
my memory. I shall learn by rote. I shall recite
every syllable, though I understand nothing.

I know
it can profit a woman to exchange her whole
destiny for a song.

4

I am capable of grief. When the cat kills birds, I bury them. When the cat dies, I bury her. When the lamb dies, and the bullock and the dressed fowl and all the fishes, I bless them before I eat. The pigs I hardly recognise, but I bless them too when they fry or bake or boil.

Lord knows what I am made of. Pain is not a metaphor, the sisters say. Pain is our necessary condition and grief its atonement.

Sybil says celebrate, but we are consumed with weeping.

5

I have buried many sisters in my time. Sweet Jasmine, who had perfect deportment and harboured men when the fires came. And Jolly Jan, for whom marriage was a breeze and childbirth a piece of cake. She never complained; it was all set before her as a vast banquet, to see how much she could devour. Then there was Little Aunt Lola, who kept herself to herself and finally got the vote. And Eglantine, whose nature like her name short-circuited desire. I was, at one time, specially fond of Jane, who chose women with such flamboyance that they excused her from work and gave her a pension. Ruth, I remember, spent her whole life laughing, even when they cut off her breasts.

I could go on. But in fairness, I must admit that I myself have eschewed rigour or discipline of any kind, being mindful of the incantations I am paid for. Let us give thanks, as is fitting, to Aphrodite, or Apollo, or mighty Artemis, by whose divine decrees/ under whose provenance etc.

I know my place.

6

Sybil, being sometimes human, is subject to torments: the paths not taken where the treasure clearly lay but what matter when the knowledge came too late . . . and the flesh (hanging and dragging, smooth only at a distance) making its dreadful demands in the dead of night and no one there or someone there but sleeping . . . and the creeping outside the house (it is only creatures it is only the wind it is only ghosts it is only old wood or walls or bits of twig it is only imaginings)

and the farmer (she is sixty now and has bad feet) says that when the cows cry all night it's because their calves have been taken away but who would be a farmer? so close to blood, so practical . . . and though my father lies below, I must join him once and for all.

Sybil, suffering a-plenty though her heart is full of gold, is a model of mendacity, asking only what is necessary. Cry; for the struggle naught availeth, and the race is already run.

7

Spin no more designs. Now we are thrifty and light-fingered at once; cautious and cavalier. I find you excellent in every way and wonderfully mannered. I shall show you off to the sisters; you exemplify their current fashion. I shall show you off to my father who is indifferent in the best sense. I shall show you off to my children if they call.

Now that passion has become portly and grand and the subject of research, I have taken up interiors and begun a boudoir. It has mirrors, of course, in gilded frames, and cushions and rugs. And I make much of satin.

8

Sybil: the women crouch now when you pass, though they used to stand and shout. There have been usurpers about, and crimes done. The women became apostate, renouncing true pleasure for the sake of gain. It's human, after all; the women so longed to be human.

And they found your rule queenly.

And they found you mysterious, dividing with your many tongues, contemplating order.

And they found you unkind when they wanted careers, or nationalism, or life in the sun.

You
were
unkind.

You whispered in my ear, "why don't they eat cake?"

Sybil's Ch/arity

I found strange ways, beyond seeing or believing.
I found contrition in the bawling waves the
$\qquad\qquad\qquad\qquad$ *frantic masts their*
$\quad$ *shivering beautiful as bells the breached sea wall*
I found compassion in the creatures frozen in the
$\qquad\qquad\qquad\qquad\qquad\qquad$ *broken cliffs*
$\quad$ *[petrus – rock: Upon This Rock;*
$\quad$ *petrus – I catalogue: fossil – This Rock;*
$\quad$ *petrus – I slay: In the Name of God Amen]*
My bones wait likewise.

Sybil is my venturing and my canopy.

1

I have lost sight of my mother she is so long dead
                                            I was
therefore abandoned though I had studied in halls
of learning where speech in those days was
judicious
         my mother was untrained my father said,
so she fussed with my hair instead; she found me
painful right from the start
                        (she herself when she
dressed for dinner could never quite carry it off
being girlish and kindhearted. Safety, she thought,
should come first)
                        So when I became a man I put
away childish things.

2

Lily the white matron launders her household linen and launders her vernacular. She has travelled widely and has a black child. There are exigencies. Pearl Bailey wouldn't go home and Virginia Woolf – hopelessly obliged – gave up the ghost. I know women, Lily confides, who sell literary estates; and other women, who write pornography. They'd go to war, if they could: slit throats, throw bombs, stuff a man's balls with sage and marjoram. And I know about racism, says Lily the white; my child keeps to herself the slings and arrows. She is rewarded in her skin for my disloyalty.

3

Sybil is able, amiable, compliant, compatible,
deliciously desirable, firmwilled, formidable.

                                                    She
makes the swans glide the length of the river and
back again; she makes the apples glint in the
trees as soft and sharp as the mirrored walls of
Rajasthan; she makes the pacific ocean tremble
with fame and awe; she gestures/she raises an
eyebrow, an arm; she

                        speaks her rich bass, deeper
than a cello; she rises and falls, empires notwith-
standing.

But who can fully know the ardour of
her thighs, given her immense audacity? Music
plays, the drama begins (but soft! who is the
hero? who the king?) the ladies settle their
skirts, the gentlemen compose the sinews of
their necks, the babies, tucked up tight back
home, dream their warm and milky dreams, the
politicians, working late, divert disaster one
more time.

                    Oh my Sybil: the world forgets us.
Come to my bed and open me.

4

All apples shine before they fall
Though the worm will thrive within
            and the sweet rain follows

I smell the honey full in the hives
I add myself whole to the harvest
            and the sweet rain follows

Though the worm will thrive within
Each apple sates us equally
            and the sweet rain follows

I add myself whole to the harvest
Incarnate from the heat of the sun
            and the sweet rain follows

Each apple sates us equally
And therefore is no murder done
            and the sweet rain follows

Incarnate from the heat of the sun
I am my sisters' proper fruit
            and the sweet rain follows

And therefore is no murder done
All apples shine before they fall
            and the sweet rain follows

5

Sybil (lover and friend) how you

tease and beguile
with the swish of your hem with the trill of your
anklets with your painted eyes! Is my following
fevered? Should I dab at my face cover my sweats
with purest silk scent myself with feminine potions
and portents? Or should I stride about like any
braggart, smelling of beer and biceps? How

formless I am
in the white heat of your stare.

But you have never
(in your infinite) you have never minded in which
guise or in which retrogression I appeared; or which
code I honoured;

and you have never minded in
which dialect I spoke.

And you have disregarded
my protestations.

6

Sybil is set upon a path. The wind blows. The berries left on the hedgerows harden in the mist. Autumn is for assessment and for anticipation of the blasted heath. But not all is lost.

I come upon the oyster-catcher in the estuary. The reeds are dank; the tourists have abandoned this year's detritus. The old woman to whom the oyster-catcher speaks (she, and only she) we call Old Sylvia. They speak, these two, alone in the shallows. The clouds are purple and yellow.

Old Sylvia in her youth knew Sybil. The bird reminds her. They could walk on mountains then and the rivers were fresh. The bird is nonchalant, even now. And I am purposed. I have heard the impossible; and it was eloquent.

7

My current injunctions (says Sybil, rueing the day)
are put out the cat at night and put out the light

because the days
shorten according to laws of perpetual motion and
therefore I must give up the perils of my unrequited
and the dangers of my unproven

(I never found
wonderful the eye of the storm where the goddesses
sit, knitting and counting and watching the blade
ascend and fall; I never found

wonderful the cry of
faith the seven oceans of hope. I was never stirred
by the beauty of the poor. I have been reticent when
the subject was revolution. Who, therefore, must
pay? Like you, I had my own heart for an offering,
but I was already pledged.)

I excuse myself.

I have
no place at your table, though you meant well to
invite me. I am too long in the tooth to argue the
merits of passion and order. I think already about
history and cost-benefit analysis.

My sisters wanted
what was best for me. (I find wonderful a friend's
hand, resting on a table, a book, a head, a breast.)

8

I, Sybil, make out of ashes what I please to make: place or pattern, sign or symmetry. You, my sisters, have done nothing other. I have heard you, singing and weaving, sewing and cleaving, planning and reckoning.

There are more than two sides to the question; and there are more than two questions.

Did you really want justice?

I have wanted the sun-scattered sea, the easy limbs of a lover, the shelter of tree ferns flourishing.

Justice was the last thing on my mind.

9

Old Sylvia is sifting her remorse. On one side are her photographs; on the other, her handful of letters. Do the words tell best? Or the frozen faces? She is on her knees. Her hair is falling out. She sleeps in a single bed, remembering the mares she had. We were all young once, and had tight bellies, and beliefs.

(Are you watching me, Sybil? Do you see how I'm full of feeling for Old Sylvia? Do you remark how I suffer her silence? Do you acknowledge how I revere experience?)

(Are you pleased with my obeisance?)

I have called in a professional nurse to deal with the incontinence. And I've written you a letter, Sybil, setting out my defence.

10

Sometimes Sybil slides about on her belly, curious to feel the shapes of seducing. She learned how to do this in drama therapy.

You should take what you want, hissed Sybil, practising. The air is blameless, and the vegetation, and all the froth of the earth.

You are playing with fire, Sybil admonishes herself, meditating now. They burnt Joan and the others for gabbling and babbling; and they burnt the Asians for speaking in strange tongues.

Sybil falls silent. It is impossible to pre/sent the facts. All the sacred texts, after all, were written by human hands.

Patient Among Apples
An Afterword

Suniti Namjoshi

*It is necessary to make pilgrimage. Being anciently
outcast, we heard what was in the air, felt the sun
on the crumbs of Delphi, saw olives and cypresses
flare.* (I, 1.)

As lesbians we know we have a past. As lesbians
we are becoming aware that we also have a literary
tradition; but establishing such a tradition is not
easy. Women, and particularly lesbians have been
systematically silenced; and even when we have
managed to write at all our work has been obscured,
obliterated, or ignored and the indisputably lesbian
elements have been pronounced irrelevant. Often
self-preservation has forced us to write in code.
Facts have been made inaccessible or simply lost.
Clearly the lesbian literary historian is engaged in a
colossal and exhilarating task. It is what she contributes to the building of a lesbian culture; but it is
not a task that we can leave to the specialist alone.
We, as ordinary lesbians who read and write and

think about what it means to be lesbian, have our share in it too. The building of a culture is a process and each of us is a participant in this process. It is not just the books that are offered to us that constitute this culture, it is what we make of the books that really matters. (It's worth noting that what other cultures make of our books also matters, not only to us, but to them as well.)

If we as lesbians are to understand our own work, our very selves, then we have to continue to make our own tradition – I am about to say something odd – we have to be able to *make* our own past. The past is not just a set of facts. It is a set of selected facts. And a tradition is not just a set of selected facts. It is an interpretation of a set of selected facts. When men do the selecting, it is this limited selection that is offered to us. Lesbians discover that there's very little there that records our own knowledge, experience and point of view. We are therefore faced with first having to find the facts that we can choose from: an enormous cultural task which involves a re-*vision* by lesbian historians, social scientists, philosophers, artists, critics and other commentators and in which the lesbian community participates. Without a community a culture cannot thrive. Without a culture that accepts responsibility and is constantly engaged in the task of re-vision and re-evaluation neither a community, nor the world, can thrive.

What I have said is not really odd after all. Every writer, every person, creates her own past to some extent, even if her choice is to accept large portions of someone else's version of *their* past. The realisation that one has chosen someone else's past without making it one's own leads to alienation. Because alienation is hard to live with, it isn't surprising that many heterosexual women and even some lesbians identify themselves unthinkingly with a patriarchal past. This helps to explain why we sometimes collude in our own oppression. But when we do not collude, when instead we ask questions like, "How is this relevant to me as a lesbian? How does this fit in with what I know of the lesbian past? What does this mean in terms of what I know of the lesbian experience?" then we are engaged in the process of building a lesbian culture. And there is also the further question: if the assertion of lesbian identity does *not* require the annihilation of the rest of creation, then what is the lesbian perspective on the history of "man" and of lesbians and what is the lesbian vision for the welfare of the world?

A lesbian book, written and published under patriarchy, is in the same position as a lesbian person. Some notion of a lesbian past is necessary if the book is to be read on its own terms. For us this means that it is essential to see a lesbian work in a lesbian context and in a lesbian tradition, even though such a context and such a tradition can only be sketched in at present. What I propose to do here is juxtapose *Sybil* with some of the work of three major writers: Sappho, Virginia Woolf and Adrienne

Rich; and to ask two simple questions: 1. What has Gillian Hanscombe done in *Sybil* that they also did? 2. What has Gillian Hanscombe done that is different from what they did? That *Sybil* happily bears such comparison is, in my view, a measure of just how important this work is to lesbian literature, and *therefore* to literature in general.

Who is Sybil?

Sybil is the lesbian prophet and archetype. But for such a prophet to come into existence, certain conditions are necessary. Some are obvious: a printing press, a publishing house . . . . Others perhaps are less so: an audience, a sense of the past and a sense of belonging. We have by now a shadowy outline of the development of these conditions. For example, some people find it important to say that Sappho had a male lover called Phaon, others stress the fact that she had a daughter, and still others insist that what's specially significant is that she had a poetry school. What everyone would agree about, should the question arise and be regarded as relevant, is that she had no printing press. For lesbians this matters because it means that much of her work has been lost. Virginia Woolf had a press; even an audience. *A Room of One's Own* (1928) consists of lectures addressed to students at Newnham, but I agree with Adrienne Rich that Virginia Woolf is "acutely conscious – as she always was – of being overheard by men" ("When We Dead Awaken: Writing as Re-vision" [1972] in *On Lies, Secrets and Silence*.) Adrienne Rich herself writes as a lesbian for other lesbians. Others, if they wish, may overhear; but she doesn't alter her tone for their benefit. Adrienne Rich precedes Gillian Hanscombe, and the audience and the consciousness that Adrienne Rich has helped to create, is one that Gillian Hanscombe can take for granted. The point is not so much that no male human or heterosexual woman may read this book and derive pleasure and profit from it; but that they cannot do so while remaining entrenched in their negation of lesbians.

In S*ybil*, Sybil speaks about and for and to a whole people, the lesbian people. To be the voice of her people is literally "Sybil's Calling," the title of Section I; she is their prophet and their archetype. Today at Delphi on Mount Parnassus only a rock remains to remind us of the original Sybil. Most of the ruins belong to the cult of Apollo, whose oracles, it is said, were delivered through a priestess who was merely his vehicle. *The Oxford Classical Dictionary* says Sibyl was originally "a single prophetic female," but as a result of being variously localised – she appeared everywhere – there were at one time as many as ten Sibyls. The irony of all this can hardly escape a lesbian consciousness. *The Oxford Classical Dictionary* goes on to say that Sibyl acquired "a position in Christian literature and art similar to that accorded Old Testament prophets."

In *Sybil* it is made clear that Sybil, as the archetypal lesbian prophet, goes on surviving and can always be heard.

They said she was theirs, that she spoke their words, that she spoke for them; but we knew just the same. She comes twice in our lives: in our preknowing and in the confirmation. (I, 5.)

This is not to say that *Sybil* is suggesting that our problems are over, the outlook is good, and that there's such a thing as progress in history. That isn't the point. What *Sybil* contains is the assured knowledge that lesbians have always existed, do exist, and will survive.

Sybil knows *all* our experience – as young women, as grandmothers, as children, through the different periods of oppression and the different modes and attitudes – because she contains it.

There were people all about, but they were all fish. There were buildings, all made of water .... When Sybil went to Parnassus, she was thirty-three; and not yet a grandmother. (I, 2.)

This conflation of different points in time is, in my view, characteristic of prophecy. Sybil is made possible only because of the lives of all lesbians. In other words, Sybil can speak as a prophet only because Sappho and Virginia Woolf and Adrienne Rich and all the others have spoken in her other voices.

Sybil's Fellow Women

Lesbians care about their fellow women, they actually like them. What? All women? All the time? No, nothing so sentimental. What's important is that there is a fellow-feeling that opposes the misogyny and the annihilation of women that is so deeply embedded in the patriarchal tradition. Sappho celebrates the women she loves, knows that the goddess is on her side: has Aphrodite say *"Who wrongs you, Sappho?"* ("To Aphrodite"). Virginia Woolf points out that the fact that "Chloe liked Olivia" really matters and that its literary implications are far-reaching. (Chapter V, *A Room of One's Own*). Giving such a statement its full resonance makes possible a literature in which relations between women are central. And Adrienne Rich articulates what we have always known about the social and political context we inhabit: *two women sleeping/ together have more than their sleep to defend.* ("The Images" in *A Wild Patience Has Taken Me This Far*, 1981). The lesbian world view is radically different from the male-centred view (especially in the West) in which man is central and everything else is the other. In the lesbian view, the lesbian is central and the woman she addresses, the other, is not other at all: they are part of each other. Sybil's entire world, past, present and future is woman-centred. *She whom I honour, honoured me. Therefore I speak . . . . Love is a discipline, she told me; and must be learned.* (IV, 2.)

The last three sections of *Sybil* explore the implications of sisterhood for the rest of creation, for pigs that are eaten, for cows that are coaxed, and for the self-confessed patriarchs, who plead, after all, a failed and therefore common humanity. *See, says my father . . . . Not the bloodline, you may understand, nor superstitious laws – but the fellow-feeling, don't you see?* (VI, 9.)

Sybil's Voice

I've said that Sybil includes and transcends all of us. Sybil can't necessarily be relied upon to be kind like Sappho's Aphrodite. She isn't necessarily wise. She isn't even necessarily moral as is claimed for the archetypal perfect man in Western religion and humanist philosophy.

Sybil said sorry said sorrily with a sweetening grace that she'd raced by the suffering sisters, turned left at the equal pay headquarters, trekked left again . . . (V, 6.)

But does that mean that every lesbian who speaks, speaks as Sybil, for Sybil? In a sense, yes; but Sybil herself has a distinctive voice. It's the voice of prophecy. All our voices echo in hers. The poem I've just quoted ends with the lines:

I want said Sybil (sorrowful as sunlight on a virgin land) more than altarfire and general commination/or, the logic of repair: I want a genuine despair. (V, 6.)

Prophecy not only includes what has been and will be; but also how things have seemed to be and how they might be. Where there is genuine despair, there is also vision. The two must go together.

To my ears, Sappho's voice is the "personal" voice of pure lyric poetry; in the context of a lyric poem she celebrates individual women. Virginia Woolf's voice in *A Room of One's Own* is the voice of polemic, however carefully modulated and ironised; she tries to explain to the young women just how and why patriarchal structures are so harmful to them, and what it is they must do to help themselves. Even *Three Guineas*, 1938, which purports to be an answer to a man, carries its direct message for women, together with an underlying message for men, if they have ears to hear. Adrienne Rich's voice is the voice of the poet who has understood that the personal is the political; the celebration of lesbian love is counterpointed by the awareness that it is a subversive and therefore dangerous political act. Every poet's work includes these elements – the lyrical, the polemical, the political and prophetic – in varying degrees; but a strong prophetic voice is relatively new in lesbian history.

Why has it arisen now? I can only offer my own speculations. I think it's because a prophet has to have a people in order to be a prophet, and we are just beginning to be a people. It's our suffering, our humiliations, our aspirations, our rage, our desires, our triumphs, our patience and our endurance that echo in Sybil. And beyond pain and humiliation there is also the reckoning for our sins, including the sins of escapism and abdication, and for the refusal to grow up and to take responsibility for anything, given our conventional defence that we are more sinned against than sinning.

The poems in Section II, "Sybil's Saturation," recount the history of our humiliation and the anger generated: *"Yes doctor we admit"; "Let's abolish"; "No beasts ourselves"*. This section voices the experiences we have all been saturated by, together with the anger and bitterness they have engendered. It also contains a steadfast refusal to be defined solely in terms of what has been done to us by others.

No beasts ourselves, we live among beasts . . . we've learned to tread lightly, to tunnel in burrows, even to fly . . . . We walk upright, feel tall; and hide with dignity. (We've discussed the choice: to be brave and flayed or be coiled and craven, spat upon, patient among apples.) (II, 7.)

Section III, "Sybil's Passacaglia," embodies this history in the treatment the prophet herself has received. Lesbians, who attempt to speak for themselves and their sisters, are silenced, ridiculed, ignored; or used and abused.

Sybil prefers, when permitted, to shun the spotlight. She knows, better than we've been taught, the problems of prophecy, the splendour of stardust. Women who walk tall are liable to be brought low and made to service the gods . . . . When she mutters under sulphur, Sybil rehearses the voices of millions. (III, 1.) ('Passacaglia' refers to a form in Western musical convention in which there are continuous variations based on a clearly defined melodic phrase which is repeated persistently, usually in the bass, but which may sometimes be transferred to an upper voice. Similarly Sybil's rumblings form a base line as a continuing reference for the variations of lesbian utterance.)

A prophet may not be honoured by her people, may be forgotten, may, like Cassandra, not be believed; but nonetheless a relationship exists between a prophet and her people. She voices their experience, their past and their future, their despair and their visions.

"The Prophetical Songs" in Section IV celebrate our lives, loves, passions, saying what we have always said to one another in different ways, in different moods: flamboyant and earthy, lyrical and respectful. They are our songs of praise.

Your bow-arm is stronger than an olive-stump, though your hands are as smooth as plums. When you pour libations, my ears sting with the brim and swish of your words. (IV, 3.)

Or, in a different mood:

The sea breasted herself, reared, fell, and was fooled. Later, she lay flat and brooding. If I had a grain of greatness in me, I'd call her a god and be glad. (IV, 5.)

Or, in mild mockery:

Want to let fly, little hushabye, while the bird's on

the wing? Will you try anything? Or pretend to rest easy? (IV, 10.)

The Sound of Sybil

Sybil speaks in different voices, and the voices combine to form the strong central voice of prophecy. That is what makes *Sybil* so extraordinarily musical. The chief source of resonance derives, I think, from the very nature of the prophetic mode. Prophecy combines everyday matter-of-fact experience with possibility, and despair with hope. These four strands are almost always simultaneously present in the sound of *Sybil* and correspond – if I am not being too fanciful – to four simultaneous lines of music. Perhaps I can demonstrate this more clearly from a few lines chosen at random:

Some people will believe anything: Adam and Eve, quantum theory, the rights of the rich. There are priests, of course, and military technicians, looting and lying. (It may not be moral and we're sorry for our sins, but at least they're natural.) (V, 2.)

Some people will believe anything is the voice of experience, but hints ironically at possibilities. The list of things that people will believe in multiplies the shifting ironies. Some people will believe in Adam and Eve because they want to, would like to; the story offers a satisfactory self-explanation. But what about the metaphysics of scientific theory?

Implausible though they might seem, at least there is no apparent self-interest. The reasons for believing in the rights of the rich (particularly on the part of the rich) are more obvious. Lesbians have not only been fed lies, they have been force-fed them. *There are priests, of course, and military technicians, looting and lying.* This is said in a matter-of-fact tone, undercutting despair. It's the voice of experience. And the moral possibilities – here impossibilities – for lesbians? If they are impossibilities, then all one can do is express regret. But in that last phrase, *at least they're natural,* there's genuine possibility again, perhaps even a glimmer of a more natural world, as well as irony, of course, since being unnatural is one of the charges levelled against lesbians.

That was an attempt to catch some of the reverberations and modulations in only four lines of *Sybil.* The double and triple ironies and the shifts in tone are echoed in changes in speed and pitch and phrasing and the patterns of stress and assonance; and precision is maintained through a very wide range of reference from the King James Bible through Shakespeare and Hopkins to popular songs. But these modulations and shifts occur within the constant presence of two sets of polarities: innocence and experience, hope and despair. And the constant presence of these polarities is precisely what defines the prophetic voice. (It is perhaps worth remarking that the formulation of polarities in just this way probably requires a Judaeo-Christian background.)

The Nature of Prophecy

Prophecy isn't polemics. The prophet doesn't argue. She says, "This is so." And that "is" has a special meaning. Prophecy isn't history, or sociology or even meteorology. Questions like, "But don't the characteristics of a lesbian change from period to period?" or "Is it possible to verify the truth of her prophecies?" or even "What large-scale events is she prophesying exactly?" don't have much meaning in this mode, because it isn't based on sequential time or on cause and effect. This mode exists in the present. The past and future are both known and encompassed. They are present in any moment of time. Cassandra said, "Troy will fall." She may have also said, "It will rise again." She wasn't believed. She wasn't treated like a prophet or even like a person. (She was treated as spoils of war.) If you switch modes and try to take a prophecy literally, you either get nonsense or you get a truism. The prophetic state-ment is eternally true; it does not belong to time in the sense that we ordinarily understand time. The prophet does not deduce events like a meteor-ologist or a racecourse bookie or even a stock-broker with the aid of a computer. I think what happens is that the past and the future are embodied in the present, as are the visionary and the everyday.

The mode includes tentative visions like Adrienne Rich's of the long-awaited woman, who is *at least as beautiful as any boy/ or helicopter* ("Snapshots of a Daughter-in-Law" 10, 1963), or Virginia Woolf's description of the first faltering steps of a new kind of woman writer (Chapter V, *A Room of One's Own*). In the prophetic mode, what has been and will be *is*. It is real. It is also *imagined*. And the two are one. In other words, the mode includes possibility and redemption as well as the despair arising from the logic of experience. Here is a description of Sybil in which what has been, can be, ought to have been, may be, should be and shall be, meet:

After abolition, Sybil may come. She is a girl. She is a dragon. A dragongirl. Sybil is a grandmother, aged forty-nine. Her daughters are aged twenty-eight. Sybil is a goat. An experienced she-goat. She is a trademark. A hard sell. Sybil has always been all-girl. When she is young, she flies like a sphinx, she roars like a lioness in the circles of the stars. Often she runs her kingdom from coffeeshops . . . (IV, 1.)

The title of Section V, "Sybil's Pre/texts," tells us clearly that Sybil's texts, our texts, have always been there; have sometimes been obscured, sometimes coded, but they are, they endure.

Sybil named the stars we see, a billion light years back . . . (V, Epigraph.)

In keeping with the paradoxical nature of this mode, it is entirely appropriate that Sybil's texts should be books of prophecy. The paradox only arises because we use the finite tenses of language for the purposes of description. In the prophetic mode redemption can be said to belong to the future, but this isn't a sequential future. Redemption is always both present and possible.

All things generally await redemption. The daffodils particularly now are sorry . . . . Sybil weeps to know such trumpetings. (V, 8.)

In these lines the constant presence of polarities is particularly clear. The daffodils belong to the world of innocence, perhaps ignorance. They make Sybil weep, because she views them from the perspective of experience. But the daffodils also give rise to hope and despair, because they are trumpets as well, they are heralds. The possibility of redemption is a constant presence. And beyond all this there is the further suggestion that the trumpetings can be heard as a celebration of the fact of redemption.

What prophecy offers is the knowledge of the past and future in the present, the knowledge of our suffering and of our hope of redemption. If we, as a people, refuse to listen to our prophets, then we must lose ourselves: not because we haven't listened to a particular warning, but because we haven't *listened* – to our own voices, to our own experience, to what we know and have always known though we are not necessarily aware of it. If it's true that Sybil needs us, needs her people, then it's also true that we need her, though we may not like it when Sybil rebukes us.

Sybil: the women crouch now when you pass, though they used to stand and shout. There have

been usurpers about, and crimes done. The women
became apostate . . . . And they found you unkind
when they wanted careers, or nationalism, or life
in the sun. (VII, 8.)

The poet as prophet also has a moral function.
The compassion that runs through Adrienne Rich's
poetry testifies to this. The question how to avoid
war at the start of *Three Guineas* is not just a
pretext for the rest of the text; it is an acceptance of
responsibility for change. And the four rules of
poverty, chastity, derision (in the sense of a refusal
"of all means of advertising merit"), and freedom
from unreal loyalties, that Virginia Woolf sets out
in Chapter II, are a means of preserving integrity.
The final sections of *Sybil*, "Sybil's Aggregation",
"Sybil"s Reckoning" and "Sybil"s Ch/arity" make
it clear that the facts of victimisation and of relative
powerlessness cannot and do not do away with the
need for moral responsibility for oneself and for
the world. Were it otherwise, questions of morality
would apply solely to an Omnipotent Being. Were
it otherwise, our status as lesbian-victims would
doom us to a status of moral, or rather, amoral
infancy in our own eyes.

I, Sybil, have put no torch to living flesh and am
therefore guiltless. Being incapable makes me
unculpable. (VI, 3.)

Having it stated like that makes us admit in our
hearts that that is not true, that it is no more true of
us as "harmless" lesbians than it is of chest-thumping
patriarchs, who, after all, only lived a little, went

"roaming in the gloaming", "had hearts as strong as horses", "bred like bulls", "wept with pride" at the sight of their own brotherhood and died in the end as must we all (VI, 4).

And are we so harmless anyway?

Remind me, Sybil, how the women flocked to overcome, but how – being birds of a feather – they fought over every crumb. (VII, 3.)

Surely there must be a reckoning?

I am capable of grief. When the cat kills birds, I bury them. When the cat dies, I bury her . . . . The pigs I hardly recognise, but I bless them too when they fry or bake or boil. (VII, 4.)

And is grief the same thing as compassion or charity, particularly when not acted upon? Is the love of women the same thing as love or charity for the world?

Sybil (lover and friend) how you tease and beguile with the swish of your hem . . . But you have never (in your infinite) you have never minded in which guise or in which retrogression I appeared . . . (VIII, 5.)

Is confession enough?

I was never stirred by the beauty of the poor. I have been reticent when the subject was revolution. (VIII, 7.)

And would that have been the answer? Morality isn't easy *All the sacred texts, after all, were written by human hands.* (VIII, 10.) But the need to take on moral responsibility, to accept that we do, in fact, have moral stature, that in the final section of

Sybil is a clear injunction.

It is the duty of the prophet to lay down the law, or to phrase it differently, to remind us again and again, that the law is love.

Sybil is set upon a path. The wind blows. The berries left on the hedgerows harden in the mist. Autumn is for assessment and for anticipation of the blasted heath. But not all is lost . . . (VIII, 6.)

Sybil's voice can be heard in the land. She was never lost. She always returns – *over and over and over*. Poetry matters. Today there are lesbian poets writing all over the world, their work some of the finest that has ever been written. Like Nicole Brossard in her poem, "Ma Continent," we can each keep adding to our list of lesbian poets, confident in the knowledge that by now the list is open-ended. Each time we do this, we also participate in the making of our own culture and in the re-making of the world.

Suniti Namjoshi
October 1991, Devon.

SPINIFEX PRESS

is a new independent publishing venture that publishes innovative and controversial feminist titles by Australian and international authors. Our list includes fiction and non-fiction across a diverse range of topics with a radical and optimistic feminist perspective.

Spinifex Press won the international Pandora New Venture Award, 1991.

OTHER SPINIFEX TITLES

International anthology

Angels of Power
and other reproductive creations

edited by Susan Hawthorne and Renate Klein

ISBN: 1-875559-00-0

An Australian Feminist Book Fortnight Favourite,
1991

The first collection of drama, short fiction and poetry on reproductive technology, IVF, genetic engineering and surrogate motherhood. In the tradition of Mary Shelley's *Frankenstein*, the writers in this book use technological developments as their starting point in tracing the consequences of reproductive technologies. Imagination, vision and a good joke come together and demonstrate that women can resist the power of god-like scientists who long to create monsters and angels.

'*Angels of Power* is an important ground-breaking anthology . . .' Karen Lamb, *Age.*

'*Angels of Power* should head the reading list of any course in ethics and reproductive technology.' Karin Lines, *Editions.*

'. . . renders ethical issues imaginatively through fiction and contributes significantly to this important debate.' Irina Dunn, *Sydney Morning Herald.*

Health

RU 486: Misconceptions, Myths and Morals

Renate Klein, Janice G. Raymond and Lynette J. Dumble

ISBN: 1-875559-01-9

Human Rights Award, Certificate of Commendation (Non-fiction) 1991

A controversial book about the new French abortion pill. The authors examine the medical literature on the drug, including its adverse effects. They evaluate the social, medical and ethical implications, including the use of women for experimental research, in particular third world populations, and the importance of women-controlled abortion clinics. The book is excellent case study material for medical, health and women's studies practitioners and students.

The authors are experts in feminist ethics, women's health and medical science.

Co-published in the US with the Institute on Women and Technology, MIT, Cambridge, MA, USA.

Feminist crime fiction

Too Rich

by Melissa Chan

ISBN: 1-875559-02-7

'You can never be too thin or too rich,' said Wallis Simpson, Duchess of Windsor.

But Francesca Miles, independent feminist detective, disagrees. When one of the richest men in Sydney is found dead in his penthouse she teams up with Inspector Joe Barnaby in a mystery that follows the trials and tribulations of a family that should have everything money can buy.

A thoroughly riveting read. This is crime fiction at its best.

'. . . an intelligent and politically interesting plot.' Venetia Brissenden, *Mean Streets*.

'Hooray for Melissa Chan and may she write many more whodunnits.' *WEL-Informed*.

' . . . an immensely entertaining read.' *Ita*.

Quiz book

The Spinifex Book of Women's Answers

by Susan Hawthorne

ISBN: 1-875559-03-5

Who was the first writer in the world? What was the name of the first novel ever published? What was the name of the woman God made before making Eve? Who was the first woman to make a million dollars? Who wrote *The Autobiography of Alice B. Toklas*? Who wrote the first convict novel in Australia? Who invented the wheel? Who did Einstein's mathematics? Who started the Russian Revolution with the cry 'Bread and Roses'?

All were women. When the next person asks you: Where are all the famous women painters/composers/ writers/scientists? – this book will help you show exactly who many of them were. A great gift book for teenagers and adults.

Fiction

The Falling Woman

by Susan Hawthorne

ISBN: 1-875559-04-3

The Falling Woman memorably dramatises a desert
journey in which two women confront ancient and
modern myths, ranging from the Garden of Eden to
the mystique of epilepsy, and the mysteries of the
universe itself. In the guise of three personae – Stella,
Estella, Estelle – the falling woman struggles to find
the map for her life and meet the challenge of her own
survival.